THE WAR WITHIN THESE WALLS

Written by **ALINE SAX**

Illustrated by **CARYL STRZELECKI**

Translated by **LAURA WATKINSON**

Eerdmans Books for Young Readers

Grand Rapids, Michigan • Cambridge, U.K.

It was September 1939 when the Germans invaded our country. A month later, they marched into Warsaw and took up residence as if they would never leave.

The war seemed to be over. But after the dust of the bombings had settled, a very different war began . . . a war against some of us.

It started with harassment, humiliation.
Every day, people were stopped, shot,
beaten to death,
kicked to death,
hounded to death,
frozen to death.
Death became everyday life.

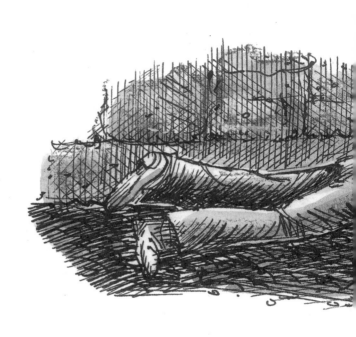

The Germans laughed while the bystanders remained silent.

Then the posters came.
The individuals became an entire group.
An entire people.

ALL JEWS OVER THE AGE OF TEN ARE REQUIRED TO WEAR A WHITE ARMBAND WITH A BLUE STAR OF DAVID ON THE RIGHT SLEEVE OF THEIR OUTER GARMENTS. DISREGARDING THIS ORDER WILL BE PUNISHED BY IMPRISONMENT.

ALL JEWISH STORES AND BUSINESSES MUST BE CLEARLY MARKED.

IT IS FORBIDDEN FOR JEWS TO CARRY MORE THAN 200 ZLOTY IN CASH.

NON-JEWS MAY NOT DO BUSINESS WITH JEWS OR SHOP IN JEWISH STORES.

JEWS MUST DECLARE ALL OF THEIR BELONGINGS.

IT IS FORBIDDEN FOR JEWS TO MAKE USE OF TRAINS OR MOTORIZED VEHICLES.

Possessions, houses, women were requisitioned.

———————————————

I had to wear an armband, too.
I was no longer allowed to go out with my friends.
I was not permitted to sit with them on a bench or to
play soccer in the park.

l had never felt so Jewish before.

After that, the wall came. It seemed to appear overnight, but there must have been posters, announcements, and then construction. A small part of Warsaw, the part where we lived, was sealed off. All non-Jews had to leave. The lines on the map turned into lines of soldiers, and then lines of barbed wire. Finally it became a ten-foot-high line of bricks with barbed wire and shards of glass that marked out the sky. Jews were no longer allowed to leave and non-Jews were not allowed to enter. Now there were two Warsaws. The Jewish ghetto and the Aryan section.

Seuchensperrgebiet

screamed the signs at every gate and every opening in the wall. Out of bounds. Risk of infection.

We were not sick when the wall was built.
We became sick because the wall was built.

"Why should I stay here?"

Why didn't I rip off that blasted armband, run past the guard posts to the other side of the wall, and go on with my life, in my city, with my friends?

Father hit me. Not hard, but it was still a shock. He had never hit me before.

"We do not deny who we are!" he hissed. "This is Warsaw for us now."

Mother was silent. She missed the flowers in the park. I could see it in her eyes. She stared down at her feet.

Father's Warsaw grew more and more crowded.
Day in, day out, long lines of people streamed
into the ghetto. All of the Jews from the entire
city of Warsaw, the outlying districts, and the
villages around the city were "relocated," as the
Germans put it. All of them, within these walls.

I often used to stand at the gate and watch them. I don't know why. Those miserable figures made me so angry. They had piled all of their belongings onto a cart, or stuffed them into a suitcase. They shuffled their feet and looked at the ground. Their clothes flapped around their bodies, as if they were scarecrows. A dairyman from outside the city drove his cow ahead of him.

Endless lines of people. Carts and homemade trolleys
piled high with household goods, crying children,
sick people, old people. Throughout the ghetto
you could feel the newcomers streaming in.
They were looking for a place to live.
A room, a basement, an attic.
A dry spot among the rubble of a bombed-out house.
Like dirty water, they kept on pouring into the mouth
and nostrils of the ghetto.
Until it would be impossible for us to breathe.

Our apartment was taken over.
We carried our most precious belongings into the kitchen.
Strange voices and new smells filled the other rooms.
Strangers wormed their way into our lives
and dragged us roughly into theirs.
And, in our hallway, a woman brought a baby into the world.

All the doors were kept open.

For more light.
More air.
More noise . . .

We did not speak.

We peered into each other's lives,
yet ignored each other's discomfort.

We never became neighbors.

There were too many mouths in the ghetto. Too many empty stomachs. The ration coupons did little to help. The Germans made sure no extra food came in.

"They're trying to starve us!" people wailed in the streets. Most didn't want to believe that: "They need us. As laborers. They won't just let us starve to death."

I believed it, though. Even those in the short lines
that trickled out of the ghetto every day to work
for the Germans did not receive more food to
eat. There were so many of us. They didn't need
all of us. *Austauschbar* is what they called us.
Interchangeable. Replaceable. But I pushed those
thoughts away. I wouldn't simply allow them to
starve me. We weren't pigs in a shed waiting for
the farmer to throw us some garbage.

Everyone tried to sell everything.
Bookstalls popped up out of the ground like mushrooms.
Jewels changed hands for the price of a loaf of bread.
Heirlooms were traded without emotion.

Food.

We had to have food.

The volumes of Father's medical encyclopedia were sold off separately.
One buyer could have all the illnesses from K to N.
Another from O to R.

My little sister Janina sold her doll.
For an ounce of lard.

Those who had little soon had nothing at all. Children sat and begged beneath the packed window displays of butchers and bakers. Old people died beside carts stacked with vegetables.

Wealthy women with dead foxes around their necks looked the other way, walked on by. They went into cafés and restaurants where piano music and the tinkling of champagne flutes washed away the misery.

Until the food ran out entirely . . .

. . . and there was nothing left to buy.

The women were stuck with their dead
foxes. Their porcelain plates were empty
and their silver cutlery grew dull.
Hunger made no distinction between rich
and poor. Between young and old.
Between men and women.

People dropped down in the streets . . .

and died . . .

Relatives brought out the dead and laid
them on the sidewalk.
The funeral cart would take them.

It made me mad. Everywhere you looked, you saw people giving up. But I would not let them bring me to my knees. When hunger hollowed out my stomach, I filled myself with fury.

Father's patients sat on the kitchen table while he examined them. Mother lay on the mattress and closed her eyes as people unbuttoned their shirts and Father pretended to listen to their hearts. He knew what was wrong with them.
Always the same. Malnutrition. Typhus.
People kept coming. Even though he had no medicine left. "I can't send them away, can I?" he said with a sigh.
He had nothing for them, and they had nothing for him.

I slipped outside.
All those strange smells were suffocating me.

It was a mild day the first time I saw the parakeet on the wall. Its colors stood out against the grayness of the ghetto. I had never seen such a beautiful bird. It did not belong there. I stared at it. The noise of the ghetto, the tram passing on the Aryan side, the shouts of the German and Jewish police — they all died away. The world disappeared. The parakeet looked at me. "I don't belong here. And neither do you," it seemed to say. Then it spread its wings and flew over the wall.

Gone. With a loud bang, the ghetto returned.

If it was so easy for the bird to fly over the wall, why couldn't I do the same?

Now that the patients had stopped bringing
food, we had to make do with what we got
for our ration coupons.
It was not enough.

Janina sat slumped on a kitchen chair. She
had no energy for playing. The hunger had
taken her friends away.
She no longer laughed at my jokes.
Mother became ten years older every day.
I wanted to see her cheeks blush and her
eyes shine again.
But I couldn't help her.
She was slipping through our fingers
and we couldn't hold on to her.

We had to have food.

———————————————

I was going to get out of that ghetto.
Even if I had to fly over the wall.

For days l walked past that wall.
l observed guard posts. Looked for
gaps. Estimated distances. Studied
the windows of the houses along the
wall. Found out how much it cost to
bribe the guards at the gate.

I soon spotted a chance. Every
morning the funeral cart passed
through the city. Young men piled
up the corpses. Bony arms and legs,
heads with big dark eyes, ribs beneath
parchment skin, all twisted into a
tangle of nakedness.

Clothes were for the living.

It was astonishing how quickly you became used to the smell of starvation and the sight of naked corpses.

When the cart was full, the men pushed
the bodies to the Jewish cemetery, outside
the wall. But when the cart returned, it
wasn't empty. The men held on tightly to
the tarp, their eyes gleaming with guilt.
They quickly loaded more corpses onto the
cart. I knew what they were hiding. The
Jewish cemetery was next to the Christian
cemetery — where the Poles were giving
them food.

I sat by the roadside and studied the workers
from beneath my brows.

I made a list:
- win the trust of the Poles at the cemetery
- fool the Germans and the Jewish police
  at the checkpoint
- look for a cart and find someone who is able
  and willing to help me push it
- work out the timing
- get hold of the necessary papers

It was a hopeless list, but I didn't want to admit
that. I had to have food for Mother.

For Janina.

Then, a few days later, another opportunity
presented itself.

I was terrified the first time I went to the other side. But I was also proud. I'd thought of everything. Those Nazi pigs weren't going to stop me. I'd chosen a spot I knew well. I had a backpack with a change of clothes, a rope for emergencies, and some of Mother's rings for trading.
The only thing I didn't have was a flashlight.

l waded through the cold water in complete darkness, following the slimy wall with my hand. The splashing of the water and the squeaking of the rats drowned out every other sound.

Now and then, l stopped. Could l hear footsteps in the water? Was someone following me?

The darkness seemed to be pressing on my lungs. l had to get out of there. l had to get back to the surface. l walked faster and faster until my hand found the rusty rung of a ladder. lt would have been safer to walk on a little farther. But the stench of the sewer water and the thick darkness were suffocating me. l climbed up and slowly lifted the manhole cover. When l saw where l was, l sighed with relief. lt was the manhole in the yard of the girls' school.

l climbed out of the hole, ran to a nearby cluster of trees, and changed my clothes.

It went so smoothly. I couldn't believe it. After a few more times, I found a safer entrance and exit. On the Aryan side, there was food for the taking. I made my way through stores, hotel kitchens, the girls' school, and some private houses before finally finding paradise: a school friend's bakery. The baker never locked the basement window. I stuffed my pockets full of bread rolls and cakes. The man must have known I was going there. But I never saw him.

Father didn't ask any questions. Mother looked eagerly at the cakes and anxiously at me. Janina thought I went to the bakery around the corner every day. Their eyes shone and I stood taller. I smuggled the anger out of my body. Whenever I saw people slumped by the roadside, I wanted to pick them up and shake them. "Don't let those filthy Nazi pigs win!" I wanted to scream. But I just walked on quickly and stuffed even more cakes into my pockets.

When I came back one night, Janina was waiting by the manhole. "The baker isn't around the corner," I said and headed home.
She followed me without saying a word.
The next night she was there again.
I felt her shadow slipping after me.
Down in the sewer, I kept looking over my shoulder.
But fortunately she didn't follow me down there.

I tried to be more careful. Quieter.
But it was like she never slept.

"Go back inside," I hissed. "I'm going alone." That didn't help. No matter how quickly I walked, she ran after me.
Night after night.

The Germans knew about it. One day,
one of them decided the smuggling had
to stop. The number of guards doubled.
We had to watch out for the Polish police
outside, the Jewish police inside, and the
Germans everywhere.
They were determined. Their faces were
masks without emotion. Their eyes were
sharp and their hands were quick.

People who slipped through the gates
were shot.

Children who crawled through holes in
the wall were beaten to death.

Every day more corpses dangled from
the lampposts. With signs around their
necks.

Schmuggler –Smuggler

But we weren't going to be beaten. While the streets were still wet with spilled blood, others slipped past the gates and through the holes in the wall.

l stood behind an overturned tram. And saw a
girl and a boy quickly lowering themselves into
my manhole. l started to count. l was going to
follow them after counting to one hundred and
fifty. At thirty-eight, two Germans arrived, and
at forty-two l saw the most gruesome weapon
l had ever seen.

An all-engulfing firestorm chased
through the sewers.
I didn't hear it. I didn't see it.
But I knew what had happened.

_____

It took a count of one hundred and
fifty to reach the other side.

l dreamed. Every morning l awoke with scorched skin and burned lungs. My hands trembled and my mouth became dry when l saw the manhole cover.

"Why have you stopped going?" asked Janina.
"Because it's too dangerous," I thought.
But I couldn't say the words.
I didn't want to be a coward.
The Germans could not be allowed to win.
"I'll go," she said suddenly.
She slipped out, past the searchlights, the soldiers
and the policemen, and through the gate.

She was quick. Small. No one noticed her. Like the
parakeet on the wall, she flew out of the ghetto.
I hadn't seen the bird since that day.
But Janina came back.
And she brought pickles with her.

I said nothing to Mother.
I avoided Father's eyes.
My guilt grew and grew.
What I didn't dare to do
came as easily to her as skipping . . .

Until the day l waited . . .

and waited . . .

. . . and anxiously waited . . .

. . . slumped against a wall, and waited and waited . . .

. . . nauseously waited . . .

. . . until I could no longer stand.

The searchlights disappeared in
the gray of morning. The sounds of
daytime resumed. As the sun climbed
higher, I saw the parakeet on the wall.
"You don't belong here," I whispered.
It flew away and never came back.

Just like Janina.

I told Mother I had helped her escape. Her grateful relief weighed on my shoulders, as heavy as lead. I said nothing. I wanted to believe it myself. The other side was the safe side, wasn't it?

I had tried to take care of them.

But I had failed.

Made it even worse.

It tore me apart that I didn't dare to go look for her.

My hunger devoured me.

Mother's hunger devastated me.

But the patrols with the flamethrowers
were everywhere. Always.

Would Mother have to die because I
was scared? Because I had given up?

———————————————

Father solved the problem for me.
The Jewish Council asked him to
work at the hospital. Extra soup as
payment, they whispered.

I hated myself.

Fall came. And then winter.

l went to the wall every day.
Spring came. And then summer.
The leaves of the calendar fell to
the ground and we could not buy
a new one.
But we all knew.
It was summer 1942 when the
new posters came.

-1-

ALL JEWS IN WARSAW, REGARDLESS OF AGE OR SEX, ARE TO BE RESETTLED IN THE EAST.

-2-

THE FOLLOWING GROUPS ARE EXEMPTED FROM RESETTLEMENT:

a. All Jews who work for a German factory or for a company that carries out work for the German authorities.
b. All Jews who belong to the Jewish Council.
c. All Jews who are employed by the Jewish Hospital.

l could breathe again.
Father was allowed to stay.
And that meant Mother and l
could stay, too.

———————————————

But still l read on.

-3-

EVERY JEW MAY TAKE 15 KILOGRAMS OF LUGGAGE. VALUABLES SUCH AS GOLD, JEWELRY, MONEY MAY BE TAKEN. EVERYONE MUST TAKE SUFFICIENT PROVISIONS FOR THREE DAYS.

-4-

THE RESETTLEMENT WILL COMMENCE: JULY 22, 1942, AT 11:00 AM

-5-

PUNISHMENT:

a. Any Jew who leaves the ghetto without permission will be immediately shot.
b. Any Jew who carries out any action to disrupt the resettlement will be immediately shot.
c. Any Jew . . . immediately shot.
d. Any Jew . . . immediately shot.
e. Any Jew . . . immediately shot.

l stopped reading.

Resettlement. Resettlement. We're going to live in villages in Russia. Fresh air and wide-open fields. The ghetto was buzzing.
People carefully packed up their belongings. Finally leaving the ghetto! For blue skies and the scent of rolling countryside.

Every day, endless lines of people trudged to the station. The trains stood ready, just outside the ghetto. Suitcases were filled with exactly fifteen kilograms. People went away. And never came back.

––––––––––––––––––––––

l didn't believe the stories. l couldn't.

We're being resettled in villages in the east.

It's really true. One of my uncles sent me a postcard.
He says, "Greetings from Auschwitz. It's wonderful here!"

The whole family can stay together in Russia.
We'll be working in the fields.

The people there are very friendly.
They're expecting us.

We won't have to work on Shabbat.

German soldiers forced their way into houses,
smashed furniture to pieces,
yelled for documents.

People were pushed down the stairs.
Children were grabbed by their hair if they walked too quickly.
Old people were beaten if they walked too slowly.

The trains were freight cars.
There were no seats.
No windows.
There was no air.

Anyone who fled was shot.
Anyone who did not obey was shot.
Anyone who protested was shot.

As the ghetto emptied and the shouts and the shots still
echoed around the walls, our last hopes vanished.
Someone had returned . . .

They're taking us to camps
to murder us.

My fear was put into words.
Those words sounded even harsher from
other mouths than they had in my head.
They meant to murder all of us.

All of us.

Even those who had documents to say
they could stay were no longer safe.
For the first time in two years, I was no
longer angry.
I was scared. Scared to death. I stopped
going to the wall. I sat at the kitchen
table and stared at the emaciated body
on the mattress.
It was all that remained of my radiant
mother. Only the soft rattle of her breath
showed she was still alive. When Father
came back from the hospital, he sat
down beside her.
There was nothing he could do.
There was nothing I could do.

We were going to die.

I crept through empty rooms and deserted corridors. There must be something that the residents had forgotten.

A potato, a crust of bread, a pea?

A vehicle turned onto the street. I slipped over to the window and stared outside. I caught a glimpse into the back of a truck full of German soldiers. A woman with a baby carriage on the other side of the street tried to vanish into the wall. The truck drove on. But when it had disappeared around the corner, the engine came to a stop. The woman started to walk faster, but an order halted her dead in her tracks. A German soldier raced back into my field of vision. He gestured at the woman. Her eyes staring down at her feet, she handed him a piece of paper. The soldier didn't read it. He threw it on the ground and spat on it. The woman kneeled, but didn't dare to pick up the paper. Then everything happened so quickly.

The soldier kicked over the baby carriage. A bundle of blankets fell onto the ground and started to wail. The woman reached for the baby. The soldier grabbed the child by one leg. The child shrieked. The mother screamed. The soldier slammed the child against the wall. I closed my eyes. But I couldn't close my ears. The woman's scream was stopped by a shot.

Somewhere in the distance I heard a truck start up again and drive on.

My God.

MyGodmyGodmyGodmyGod,
went rattling through my head.

I slumped down against the wall. For how long?
A minute, an hour, a year?
When I opened my eyes, there was a young man in
the room. He was looking at me. I gasped, but I didn't
stand up.

"They're going to murder us all," I whispered.
He just kept on looking right at me.
"Not if we stop them," he replied.
His voice sounded a long way off.
"We have to fight back. Now.
They won't be expecting it."

Fight back? Against the Germans? How?
By spitting at them?
The young man read my thoughts. "We have
weapons," he said. "But we need more people.
Young, healthy people." His eyes bored into mine.
Slowly my old fury came bubbling back up.
We won't allow ourselves to be slaughtered, I'd always
thought. Would I finally be able to do something, to
take action?
"We have to do it now," said the young man, holding
out his hand. "I'm Mordechai Anielewicz."

"Our people have been fighting the enemy for over two years," he said, as we cautiously made our way through the streets. "Passively. We've provided food and shelter, we've kept the telephone lines open and intercepted messages from the Aryan side. We've organized training and cultural events. For over two years, my friends have helped the Jews in the ghetto to keep their spirits up. Now it's time for active resistance."

I pushed my hands deep into my pockets.

"The only way to give our people hope is to fight back. Do you know what they do to all those people who leave here?" He stopped and looked at me. I didn't reply.

"They send them to camps so they can murder them. They want to wipe us out. They put hundreds of people at a time into gas chambers. Death factories."

It was as though the clouds moved in front of the sun and the world turned dark and icy cold.

Gas chambers? Death factories?

"We can't just stand by and watch."

Mordechai walked on.

He led me downstairs into a basement and into another world. I could see a dozen people by the light of the kerosene lamps.

A man was teaching some girls how to assemble a pistol. Two other men were printing pamphlets with a hand press. A student explained to me that he was cobbling together a bomb. Some women were stacking up cans and packs of sugar in a corner. Here were the Jews who had not filled their suitcases with precisely fifteen kilograms and trudged willingly to the trains. Here were young people who felt and thought as I did. But they also dared to take action.

The door opened
and a German soldier came in.

———————————————

My breath caught in my throat.

"Is Fromka back yet?" the man asked in flawless Polish. Mordechai shook his head. I saw a glimpse of doubt in the soldier's eyes, but he said nothing. He looked at me and threw his cap on the table.

Mordechai introduced him to me: "Jacob, one of our spies." Jacob smiled and the weariness briefly slipped from his face. But, a moment later, he was staring anxiously at the door again.

Relief rippled through the room as a blond woman entered. She said nothing, just lifted her skirt. Three pistols were fastened around her legs with strips of fabric. Carefully, she untied them and placed the guns beside Jacob's cap on the table. When she loosened her hair, five bullets fell out. "If we have forty thousand zloty, they'll sell us a machine gun." Her tone was harsh.

It was as if my life was starting over again.
The hopelessness and the grueling drag
of the days gave way to hope. Energy
tingled through my body. I was drawn into
a secret network where we all had our
own tasks. Couriers brought messages,
food, and weapons from the Aryan side.
I learned how to shoot, make Molotov
cocktails, and identify mines. We practiced
military tactics in broad daylight without
the Germans realizing what was going on.
Jacob taught us to climb roofs and walls in
the courtyard of the brush factory.
Mordechai kept his eye on us. He gave us
a pat on the back. A wink. A smile.
He made us all brothers.
Fire burned in his eyes, and I could feel the
flames spreading.

Sometimes a courier was shot or caught.
Being caught was even worse than being shot.
For days, we would stop what we were doing
and just wait.
Was he being tortured?
Would he betray us?

———————————

But whenever someone was snatched away
from our group, we gritted our teeth and filled
ourselves with fury.

The command bunker on Mila Street had become our home. Until the day Jacob returned with darkness flickering in his eyes. He nodded. Mordechai knew the moment had come. He stood up.

"Tomorrow's the day."

"They want to clear out the ghetto for Hitler's birthday," said Jacob in a flat voice. "They're going to surround the ghetto this evening, and the action will begin tomorrow." A shiver passed through the silence of the bunker. Everyone looked at everyone else. This was the moment.

"We are going to shake our people awake.
The eyes of the world will be on us."

Mordechai's words stirred the glowing embers in my soul. We would show the world that we were not sheep with no will of our own. We were wolves, damn it. Wolves! The fire within me burned, and my fury dripped like oil onto the flames.

"This is not a fight for survival, my friends," Mordechai continued. "We are facing fearful odds. We are fighting for our honor. There are two ways to die — a worthy death in battle or a helpless death in front of a firing squad or in the gas chambers. Which will we choose?"

Mordechai fell silent.

———————————————

He seemed to be expecting a loud battle cry.
But our lips remained closed . . .
"We will die honorably. With weapons in our hands
and before the eyes of the world," Jacob said finally.
"And we'll take as many Nazi pigs with us as we can,"
I heard myself say. "Maybe then they'll recognize the
value of a human life."
My voice sounded as harsh as Mordechai's.

———————————————

Everyone had to be alerted.
Spies were sent to the Aryan side.
Tonight Mordechai would go through the plans
one last time.

Tonight.

Were we really going to die?

I walked down the street. I wanted to run, but I couldn't make the Germans and the Jewish police suspicious. So I ambled, but my heart raced and my thoughts flew.

Mother was asleep at home. Father wasn't there. Just as I'd expected. Just as it had been for weeks. They didn't ask where I kept disappearing to, why I no longer ate their soup, why there was a pistol in our oven.

I went outside and sat on the curb. The house was nearly empty by then. There were a few men hiding in the basement and a married couple who worked at the brush factory still up on the third floor. Our apartment was all ours again. But we went on living in the kitchen. The things the other people had left behind made me shiver.

Death factories . . .

_____

Would anyone ever come to claim those belongings?

When Father got home, I still hadn't worked out
how I was going to tell them. He woke Mother,
and I waited for them to finish their soup.
"Father, there's going to be an uprising."
He looked at me, his face almost impassive.
I told him about the day I met Mordechai.
About the preparations.
And the Germans coming to surround the ghetto.
But I didn't tell him there was little chance of
surviving the uprising.
Even a small chance is still a chance. Right?

———————————————

Father looked anxiously at Mother. But he felt
admiration for Mordechai. And for me.
"My respect," he said.
"There are bunkers and fortified hiding places
throughout the city. There's room for you."
Mother didn't want to go. She wanted to stay
at home. I desperately looked at Father for his
support. He nodded almost imperceptibly. "You
go ahead, my boy," he said, and his eyes told me
he would persuade her. I repeated the address of
the place where they could hide.
"See you soon," I said. And I headed back
outside.

If you don't say goodbye, you'll see each other again.

We were up on the roof of a house on Gesia Street. Fromka kept her eyes and our machine gun focused on the gate. A friend of hers had three ammunition belts at the ready. My pistol was tucked into my belt. On the edge of the roof were seven glass bottles filled with gasoline.

It was going to be a sunny spring day. On the other side of the wall it was Palm Sunday. The flowers in the park would be the same color as the skirts of the women and the dresses of the little girls.

I swallowed, but my throat
remained dry, and the knot
in my stomach seemed to be
getting tighter and tighter. All
night, reports about the Germans
encircling the ghetto had flowed
into the command bunker. Over
and over again, we had pored
over the map of the ghetto and
adapted the plans to the reports
we'd received. Mordechai had said
we should rest, but no one had
listened.

I took the binoculars and scanned
along the wall. The parakeet was
nowhere to be seen.

I heard the order before I saw the gate open.
In lines of four, the soldiers marched into the ghetto,
black boots echoing and runic symbols gleaming.
Two armored cars brought up the rear.
I dripped a little more fury onto the fire and reached
for my pistol.

We waited.

We waited some more.

_____

The tension slowly stretched out.
Until it was ready to snap.

The gate closed behind the soldiers. Fromka
counted down slowly. At zero, the world came
to an end. Fromka fired. On the roof opposite,
guns blazed. Soldiers dove down. Stunned.
Astounded.
Some of them fired back at nothing.

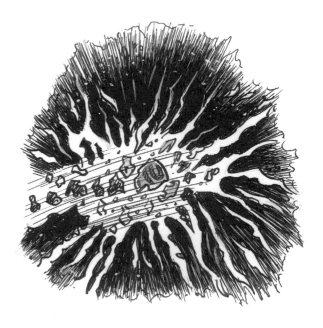

All over the ghetto, people heard the sound of
resistance.
I took one of the bottles from the edge of the roof
and set fire to the piece of cloth in its neck.
I went onto one knee and I hurled it.
I forgot to duck back down. One of the armored
cars turned into a fireball. Living torches
staggered away. Soldiers screamed.
My face glowed.
But it wasn't from the heat of the fire.

We hadn't even used up all of our bottles and bullets by the time the soldiers suddenly withdrew. They stayed away for almost two hours. They came back at eight and again at twelve. Both times they left the ghetto bloody and bowed.

That night for the first time in four years there
was not one single German in the ghetto.
We had won. I couldn't say the words. But
you could read them on every face. We had
fought. And we had won.
Two flags flew on the house above the
command bunker on Mila Street.
A Polish flag and a Jewish one.
For all the world to see.

The next morning the Germans came back.
Now it was not their boots that pounded,
but their artillery. They knew the sheep
had become wolves.
Mordechai smiled bitterly. They finally saw
us as real enemies. He gave the orders and
we set off. To locations all over the ghetto.
In small groups or alone.
I ran from doorway to doorway. I climbed
over garden walls and ran over roofs. I
hurled fire and let off shots.
But we could no longer chase them away.
We could only make sure they felt unsafe
in the ghetto. And scared.
We did not take their lives. We did not take
the ghetto. What we took was their feeling
of superiority.

We fought. For days.
We fought as no Jew had fought before.
But it was not enough.
Not nearly enough.
Mordechai was right.
We were not fighting to win.

_____

We were fighting for an honorable death.

The ghetto was not empty.

All of the residents who were still in hiding
were viewed as part of the uprising.
The Nazis pulled children from their beds
and dragged mothers outside.

Kicked them. Beat them. Shot them.

———————————————

I sat behind a chimney and watched.
With a now-empty pistol in my hand.

The Germans grew bolder.
We were vermin, and that was how they
would deal with us. They marched through the
streets with torches and set everything on fire.
One bullet in a flamethrower's tank would
have been enough. But bottles of gasoline
were all I had left.

When their hiding places caught fire, the
people tried to escape.
But the Germans spared no one.
A woman threw her baby out of a window on
the fifth floor. A man ran back into a burning
house when the Germans tried to shoot him.
Everywhere you could hear the roar of flames
and the screams of people. My eyes streamed
from the smoke, and my throat stung. The
stench of burning human flesh made me
nauseous.
I didn't want to watch people who couldn't be
saved. I had to fight.
To stop the Nazi pigs.

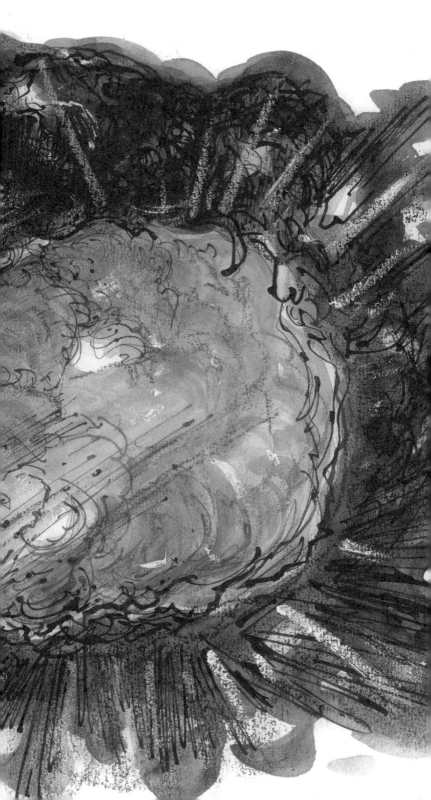

At night the flames clawed up into the sky.
The whole world saw us dying.
And did nothing.

The burning buildings forced us underground. Like mice, we darted in and out of the bunkers. We crept from basement to basement and squeezed through ventilation holes.
It was becoming more and more crowded in the command bunker. Messages were flowing in. And so were refugees. Above ground, no one was safe. Underground, there was not enough space.

For days, we fought for every bunker, for every basement. One by one, we had to surrender our hiding places. When the Germans blew up the bunkers, we had to retreat even deeper into the ground.

l knew the sewers so well that Mordechai
appointed me as the communications officer.
The title alone gave me fresh courage.
And the eyes of the others gave me
confidence. We regrouped and reorganized.
Deep under the ground.
l led small groups of our fighters from one
side of the ghetto to the other.
Our attacks became coordinated again.

But the Nazi pigs knew the sewers, too . . .

With one hand on the slimy wall, l felt my way
to the nearest exit. The hand on my shoulder
followed me. And another five hands followed
that one. No one spoke. Suddenly the hand
slid from my shoulder and the splashing of feet
behind me fell silent.

"Can you smell that, too?" said a voice,
echoing off the sewer wall. l didn't know what l
was supposed to be smelling.

"Kerosene?" the voice whispered. As though
he was uncertain. It took us only a split second
to understand what was happening.

The end of the sewer lit up, and hot air and
a roaring wind rushed toward us. At that
same moment, l felt the rungs of the ladder.
Panicking, we pushed one another to the top.

Not everyone escaped the flames.

Dazed, I walked back to the command bunker.
I had to tell Mordechai what the Germans were
doing. We needed to change our tactics.
As I was about to turn onto Mila Street, an
invisible hand pushed me back. The house
above the command bunker was surrounded by
Germans.
I crept closer, through the remains of burned-out
houses.
An officer gave an order. The soldiers put on their
gas masks.

Before long, three men came staggering out, their
hands around their throats. I ducked down. Three
shots. The coughing stopped. Then another came,
and another, and another. And each time, a shot
put a stop to the coughing.

Then it was silent.

After some time, the Germans
went inside.

When they came back out, they
had no prisoners.
Only dead bodies.

Jacob,
Lutek, one of the commanders,
and his mother.
Mordechai's girlfriend Mira . . .

I recognized them all.

They were thrown onto the ground
at the German officer's feet.

And finally, Mordechai.
His head fell on the stones with a
dull thud.

I crept between the scorched walls
and around to the back of the house.
Away from the gas and the masks.
Away from the coughing and the
shooting.

Dead.

All of them dead.

We had lost.

Mordechai had been proved right.
And yet I thought I had seen hope
flickering in his eyes, too.

Was that what an honorable death
looked like?

The two flags, which had waved so
proudly when the uprising began,
were gone.

I slumped down against the back wall
of the house. I no longer cared if the
Germans found me and shot me dead.
Or put me on a train.

———————————————

It had all been for nothing.

Someone gave my foot a kick.

My gaze moved slowly upward.

Not past a boot and a black uniform with gleaming runes. But past a skirt and blond curls.

"Misha?" said Fromka warily. When she saw I was still alive, she pulled me roughly to my feet.

"Leave me alone," I mumbled.

I'd sat down there to die.

"We have to get out of here," Fromka said curtly.

"They're dead," I said. "Everyone's dead. Mordechai and Jacob and . . . all of them. I saw it myself." She stopped tugging for a moment and looked at me. Tears had drawn white lines through the streaks of soot on her face.

"I know," she said softly. "Come on. We have to go."

"Why?"

But I didn't pull my hand away. I followed her.

"It's over. We've lost."

Fromka stopped and turned around.

Her eyes were hard.

"The others didn't die for nothing. We have to find a way out and tell everyone about them. The eyes of the world. Remember?"

I swallowed.

"But how are we going to . . ."

"Come on!"

We reached the wall without being seen.
The houses had been shot to pieces,
burned, abandoned. On the streets lay
bodies of people with no weapons.
Fromka lifted up a manhole cover and
looked at me.
"Are you ready?"
I didn't know. Could I leave all this behind?
Was there no one who needed me?
Was it really all over? I looked at the wall.
We were standing in the spot where I had
seen the parakeet for the first time. It was
hard to remember its colors.
Fromka was right.

———————————————

I closed my eyes and I flew out of the
ghetto.

HISTORICAL NOTE

Misha is a fictional character, but his story is based on true accounts of brave Jews who fought against Nazi tyranny during World War II. Warsaw's Jews were persecuted much as Misha describes in the book — and many like him really did fight and die defending the ghetto. Mordechai Anielewicz, who appears in this story as the young man who invites Misha to join the resistance, was a real person.

Anielewicz was only 23 years old when he took command of Jewish resistance forces in the Warsaw ghetto. Under his leadership, fighters made their first stand against the Nazis in January of 1943. On April 19 of that year, the Nazis surrounded the ghetto, intending to liquidate it. Armed with smuggled weapons and homemade bombs, approximately 750 Jewish fighters fought off over two thousand Nazi soldiers for four desperate weeks. Anielewicz and a number of others died when their bunker was discovered and gassed by the Germans on May 8, though a remnant of the resistance forces fought on for another week. By then thousands of the ghetto's Jews had been killed, and most of the rest captured or deported.

While the outcome of the uprising was probably inevitable, the Jewish fighters showed incredible bravery. Their remarkable story inspired others across Europe to resist the Nazis, and their suffering and courage remain a powerful witness today.

For additional information about the Warsaw ghetto uprising, visit the website for the United States Holocaust Memorial Museum at **www.ushmm.org**.

ALINE SAX is a Belgian (Flemish) author and translator. She has written a number of historical novels. Visit her website at www.alinesax.be.

CARYL STRZELECKI is a Belgian (Flemish) illustrator. He has provided art for several children's books as well as numerous newspapers and magazines.

Text © 2011 Aline Sax
Illustrations © 2011 Caryl Strzelecki
English language translation © 2013 Laura Watkinson
© 2011 Uitgeverij De Eenhoorn, Vlasstraat 17,
B-8710 Wielsbeke, Belgium

Published by arrangement with De Eenhoorn, Belgium

Original Title: de Kleuren van het Getto

This edition published in 2013 by Eerdmans Books for Young Readers,
an imprint of Wm. B. Eerdmans Publishing Co.
2140 Oak Industrial Dr. NE
Grand Rapids, Michigan 49505
P.O. Box 163, Cambridge CB3 9PU U.K.

www.eerdmans.com/youngreaders

Manufactured at Worzalla in the USA
in August 2013, first printing

19 18 17 16 15 14 13   9 8 7 6 5 4 3 2 1

Library of Congress Cataloging-in-Publication Data

Sax, Aline.
[Kleuren van het getto. English]
The war within these walls / by Aline Sax; illustrated by Caryl Strzelecki;
translated from the Dutch by Laura Watkinson.
pages cm
Originally published in Dutch by De Eenhoorn in 2011 under title:
De kleuren van het getto.
Summary: Misha and his family do their best to survive in the appalling conditions of the Warsaw
ghetto during World War II, and ultimately make a final, desperate stand against the Nazis.
ISBN 978-0-8028-5428-5
1. Holocaust, Jewish (1939-1945) — Poland — Juvenile fiction. 2. Jews — Poland — Juvenile fiction. [1.
Holocaust, Jewish (1939-1945) — Poland — Fiction. 2. Jews — Poland — Fiction. 3. Warsaw (Poland)
— History — Warsaw Ghetto Uprising, 1943 — Fiction. 4. Poland — History — Occupation, 1939-1945
— Fiction.] I. Strzelecki, Caryl, illustrator. II. Watkinson, Laura, translator. III. Title.
PZ7.S2726Co 2013
[Fic] — dc23
2013005663

The illustrations were created using pen and Chinese ink,
Conté-pencils and white pencil.
The display type was set in ATRomic.
The text type was set in ATRomic.

**Flemish
Literature
Fund**

The translation and production of this book are funded by the Flemish
Literature Fund (Vlaams Fonds voor de Letteren — www.flemishliterature.be).